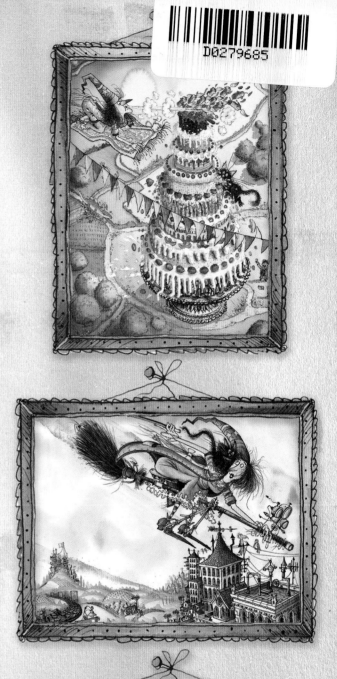

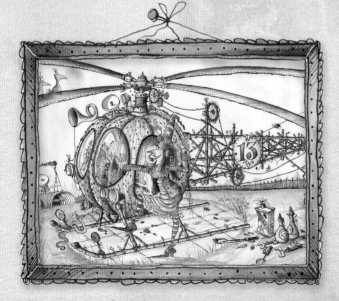

For Matt, the world record holder in reading
Winnie and Wilbur bedtime stories.—V.T.

To Sophie with love—K.P.

OXFORD
UNIVERSITY PRESS

Great Clarendon Street, Oxford OX2 6DP

Oxford University Press is a department of the University of
Oxford. It furthers the University's objective of excellence in
research, scholarship,and education by publishing worldwide.
Oxford is a registered trade mark of Oxford University Press in
the UK and in certain other countries

Database right Oxford University Press (maker)

First published in 2021

British Library Cataloguing in Publication Data available

ISBN: 978-0-19-277815-4 (hardback)
ISBN: 978-0-19-277813-0 (paperback)
ISBN: 978-0-19-277812-3 (paperback and audio)

10 9 8 7 6 5 4 3 2 1

Printed in China

www.winnieandwilbur.com

VALERIE THOMAS AND KORKY PAUL

Winnie and Wilbur
WINNIE'S BEST FRIEND

OXFORD
UNIVERSITY PRESS

Many years ago, Winnie the Witch
was a very new witch.
She had finished her lessons
at the witches' school.
She had a brand new broomstick,

a big book of spells, and a
sparkling new magic wand.

And she had a beautiful
black house in a forest.

Winnie the Witch
lived there happily.
For a while.

But it was very quiet inside
her lovely house, and Winnie
began to feel lonely.

Then she had
a good idea.

I'll ask my sisters to come and
stay with me, she thought.

Winnie had three sisters:
Wanda, Wilma, and Wendy.
They were delighted to come and stay.

They flew in on their broomsticks
with their cats and their luggage,
and Winnie wasn't lonely any more.

Winnie and her sisters had lots of fun. But sometimes they argued.

Wanda cooked dinners that Winnie didn't like.

Wilma sat in Winnie's favourite chair.

And Wendy could be very bossy.

Then one day, the three cats had a spectacular fight.

It was time for Winnie's sisters to leave.
They gathered up their cats and flew home.

It was lovely having my sisters to stay.
And now it's lovely that they've gone home,
Winnie thought.

But after a while Winnie was lonely again.
'I want someone to talk to,' she said.

Then Winnie had a good idea.
She waved her magic wand, shouted,

'Abracadabra!'

... and there was a parrot!

'Parrots are very good talkers,' Winnie said.
'SQUAWK!' said the parrot.

'Hello, parrot,' said Winnie.

'SQUAWK! SCREECH! SCREECH! SQUAWK!' said the parrot.

It flew around the room,
perched on Winnie's head,
and knocked over her best vase.

Then it flew out of the window
and back to its home in the jungle.

A parrot wasn't such a good idea,
Winnie thought. I'll have to think
of something else.
I need a friend.
But what sort of friend?

A giraffe?
Winnie loved giraffes.
No, too tall.

A cow?
The milk would be handy.
But cows are not a good idea
inside a house.

Then Winnie had a very good idea.

I know what would make an interesting friend, she thought.

She waved her magic wand, shouted,

'Abracadabra!'

... and there was a beautiful little dragon!

Winnie was delighted.
'Hello dragon,' she said.

'**Whoosh!**' went the dragon,
and Winnie's curtains were on fire.

'Oh no!' shouted Winnie. 'I forgot
that dragons breathe fire!'

She ran outside to get a bucket of water, and tripped over something on the doorstep.

Winnie put out the fire and the dragon flew back to its family in the mountains.

'Blithering broomsticks!' shouted Winnie.
'What did I fall over?'
But there was nothing there.

Winnie felt tired and lonely and miserable.
She plopped down into her favourite chair.

'MEEOOOW!

Winnie jumped up.
What was that?

There, on the chair, was a scraggly, skinny, scruffy black cat.

'**Meeow,**' it said sadly.

'Oh, you poor cat,' said Winnie. 'Don't you have anywhere to live?'

Meeooow!

Winnie found a brush and brushed the cat's fur.

Purr, purr, purr!

'Would you like a bowl of cream and some fish?' asked Winnie.

PURR, PURR, PURR!

The cat finished the cream
and fish in thirteen seconds.

It looked at Winnie.
'MEEOOOW!' it said.

'Do you want some more?'
asked Winnie.
She filled up the bowls again.

And again!

This will be a very good place to live, thought the cat. It licked out the bowls and jumped into Winnie's arms.

'Would you like to come and live with me?' asked Winnie.

'Purr, purr, purr,' said the cat.

'I'll have to think of a name for you,' said Winnie.

'Wally? No. Winston? I don't think so.
Willoughby? Certainly not!

Wilbur?
Yes! You look just like a Wilbur.'

Winnie and Wilbur
lived together happily
ever after, and Winnie
was never lonely again.

They had lots of exciting adventures.

They flew right around the world,

dived under the sea,

befriended a dinosaur,

and even zoomed up into space!

'I'm so glad you're my best friend, Wilbur,' Winnie said.

'Purr, purr, purr,' said Wilbur.